I WANNA NEW ROOM

KAREN KAUFMAN ORLOFF • ILLUSTRATED BY DAVID CATROW

G. P. PUTNAM'S SONS • AN IMPRINT OF PENGUIN GROUP (USA) INC.

G. P. PUTNAM'S SONS · A division of Penguin Young Readers Group.

Published by The Penguin Group.

Penguin Group (USA) Inc., 375 Hudson Street, New York, NY 10014, U.S.A.

Penguin Group (Canada), 90 Eglinton Avenue East, Suite 700, Toronto, Ontario M4P 2Y3, Canada (a division of Pearson Penguin Canada Inc.).

Penguin Books Ltd, 80 Strand, London WC2R 0RL, England.

Penguin Ireland, 25 St. Stephen's Green, Dublin 2, Ireland (a division of Penguin Books Ltd.).

Penguin Group (Australia), 250 Camberwell Road, Camberwell, Victoria 3124, Australia (a division of Pearson Australia Group Pty Ltd).

Penguin Books India Pvt Ltd, 11 Community Centre, Panchsheel Park, New Delhi - 110 017, India.

Penguin Group (NZ), 67 Apollo Drive, Rosedale, North Shore 0632, New Zealand (a division of Pearson New Zealand Ltd).

Penguin Books (South Africa) (Pty) Ltd, 24 Sturdee Avenue, Rosebank, Johannesburg 2196, South Africa.

Penguin Books Ltd, Registered Offices: 80 Strand, London WC2R 0RL, England.

Text set in Catchup and Tekton Pro.

The art was done in pencil and watercolor.

Library of Congress Cataloging-in-Publication Data

Orloff, Karen Kaufman. I wanna new room / Karen Kaufman Orloff ; illustrated by David Catrow. p. cm. Summary: Through a series of brief letters to his parents, Alex presents all the reasons why he should not have to share a room with his younger brother. [1. Letter writing—Fiction. 2. Brothers—Fiction. 3. Babies—Fiction. 4. Sharing—Fiction. 5. Family life—Fiction. 6. Humorous stories.] I. Catrow, David J., ill. II. Title. PZ7.O6332IP27.0332Iaw 2011 [E]—dc22 2009040106

ISBN 978-0-399-25405-5

1 3 5 7 9 10 8 6 4 2

For my editor, Susan Kochan,
who guided me and waited patiently
until I got it right. —K.K.O.

To Dad. You taught me everything I know and am. —D.C.

Dear Mom,
I know you think I should share a room with Ethan now that we have Baby Annie, but here's why I shouldn't. When Ethan sleeps, he sounds like the cat coughing up fur balls. Why can't you move Annie in with you and give me my room back?
Signed,
    Your very tired son,
        Alex

Dear Alex,
Go bother your father.
Signed,
Your very, VERY tired mother

Dear Dad,
You have no idea what it's like to share a room with Ethan! He sticks crayons up his nose and barks like a walrus! And he snores like Grandpa Ralph. So how about giving me my old room back? Please don't say, "Go bother your mother." Been there. Done that.
          Love,
            Fed-up Alex

Dear Alex,

Sorry we had to move you out of your room, but Annie's a girl, and Mom says girls need privacy to do girl stuff. I'm not sure what that is, but I'm guessing it has to do with hair and makeup.

Love,

Dad

Dear Alex,

    You know four-year-olds are a little careless. You were just like him at that age. Remember when you fell into the cake at Grandma's 60th birthday party? Good thing the candles weren't lit! Why don't you have a heart-to-heart talk with Ethan about respecting your property?

    Love,

        Dad

Dear Dad,
Thanks for the advice. Now I know exactly how to handle this.
Love,
Your diplomatic son, Alex

P.S. "Diplomatic" was one of my vocabulary words.

Dear Alex,

Do you realize you gave Ethan the side of the room that doesn't have a door? I just found him jumping up and down on his bed, yelling that he can't come out to take his bath because Alex said so. Fix this problem when you get home from soccer practice or else!

Love,
Dad

Dear Dad,

Okay, I told Trampoline Boy he can use the door now. Honestly, Dad, you see what I'm dealing with here? Please give me my room back! I promise I'll keep it really, really clean!

Love,

Neat and tidy Alex

Dear Alex,

Does that include cleaning the iguana's cage? I've noticed an unusual smell coming from that general direction. Just thought I'd mention it.

Love,

Your concerned father

Dear Dad,
   Let's not change the subject. Here's the thing. I'm practically grown-up. I wanna new room! Plus, I think I should get rewarded for all the A's I got in school.
                    Love,
          Alex the   super student

Dear Alex,

Nice try, but if I remember correctly, you got three B's and one A, and I think the A was in Lunch.

Love,

Dad

Dear Dad,

Even Stinky's dog Lurch has his own room! That dog is treated like a king. He's got six pillows and his own TV. He and Stinky watch cartoons and eat cheesy popcorn every single night. I'm not even asking for a TV. Just one little room.

Love,

Your HUMAN son, Alex

P.S. Stinky got a D in Lunch.

Dear Alex,

No can do.

Love, Dad

P.S. Stinky scares me.

Dear Dad,

It's more than the room. It's the principle of the thing! Why do I, the oldest and most important kid, have to suffer just because you and Mom had another baby? Does that seem fair? I don't think so.

Love,

Your number ONE son, Alex

Dear Alex,

Yes, you are very important to us, but so are your brother and sister. However, you make some good points. A boy your age needs his own space. Maybe we could build you a special place of your own.

Love, Dad

Dear Alex,

Slow down there, buddy! We're not gazillionaires. We can't build you a condo. I was thinking of something like a tree house. We can build it together. You won't have to share it with your brother unless you absolutely want to.

Love,

Dad

"Yessssss!"

"Thanks, Alex!"